Michael Foreman

PANDA AND THE BUNYIPS

HAMISH HAMILTON · LONDON

First published in Great Britain 1984 by
Hamish Hamilton Children's Books
Garden House, 57–59 Long Acre, London WC2E 9JZ
Copyright © 1984 by Michael Foreman
All rights reserved.

British Library Cataloguing in Publication Data
Foreman, Michael, 1938–
    Panda and the Bunyips.
    I. Title
    823'.914[J]   PZ7
    ISBN 0-241-11344-X

Originated and printed in Italy by
Arnoldo Mondadori Editore, Verona.

michael Foreman
PANDA AND
THE BUNYIPS

Panda had travelled from his home high in the snowy mountains to visit his old friend the winged Lion. They sat by the wide Limpopo River and talked of all the adventures they had shared during their travels together.

"Ah, but there's no place like home," said the Lion, lying back and looking at the stars.

"Right!" cried Panda, "but other places are different, so come on!"

"Where?" asked Lion.

"Travelling! Travelling!"

They set off next day, though not as early as Panda had hoped. The Lion felt he had to say goodbye to all his relatives *and* all his friends and all *their* relatives.

They flew from country to country
and landed for food and drink
in exotic places.

Eventually they found themselves above a country so dry and so barren that they despaired of finding anything to eat or drink. Finally, just as the light was fading, they saw a glint of water among trees at the foot of huge rocks.

The water was muddy but refreshing. They decided to stay there for the night, and hoped to find something to eat in the morning. Exhausted and hungry, they curled up together and slept.

Suddenly, a terrifying slurping and gurgling shocked them out of their slumbers. A great, dark, shadowy shape was rising out of the churning waters of the pool. It looked as though the pool had turned its slimy pocket out onto the bank. Dripping with weed and wraithed in mist, the contents were slowly forming together into the most peculiar creature never seen. It shook the weed from the end which appeared to be its head and Panda and Lion were showered with slime and little fishes. With a wet smile the creature gently flicked the little fishes back into the pool.

"G'day," he said. "You're a funny looking couple.
I'm a Bunyip, y'know."

"How do you do?" stuttered Panda
getting over his fright.
"I'm Panda and this is Lion.
We have just arrived from Africa."

"Is that so?" said the Bunyip.
"You must be hungry.
Come and eat."

He placed dripping arms around their shoulders and led them into the trees. There they fed on sweet roots and leaves, and sucked honey from drooping yellow flowers.

They talked late into the night, and Panda and Lion described their adventures.

"Tomorrow," said the Bunyip, "I too must start a journey. Sleep well, and tomorrow evening we'll leave together."

The Bunyip disappeared back into the pool, and Panda and Lion slept for the rest of the night and most of the day among the cool trees. Occasionally they were woken by a great thumping and whooshing as strange animals bounced through the trees and away over the horizon.

Just before sunset, the Bunyip returned. After a drink and more roots and honey, they set off.

For many days they followed ancient trails across the red land.

Lion was most amazed by the giant birds that ran about at great speed but never flew.

Lion flapped his wings and encouraged the big birds to fly, but they ignored him, stuck their heads out and ran even faster.

Each evening the Bunyip led them to a place of water and honey.

At last they came to a swift-flowing river. Lion, who had been taught to
swim by the Limpopo hippos, plunged in.

Panda climbed onto the Bunyip's back, and together they floated off downstream.

They were swept along by the current. Other small rivers joined the main stream, and from these rivers came other Bunyips, old and young. They bobbed up and down and greeted one another as they formed a whole flotilla of Bunyips.

"Where are we going?" whispered Panda into the Bunyip's ear.

"To the sea," replied the Bunyip. "We're going to meet up with our distant cousins. We do it every thousand years or so. We like to keep in touch."

The river was now a bobbing mass of Bunyips, and when they were finally
swept out into the bay, the sea erupted with whales and diving dolphins,
and a vast congregation of serpents.

At night, the searchlights of creatures from the deepest oceans joined the stars to the shining sea, and silver flying fishes flashed and dived among all the weird and wonderful friends.

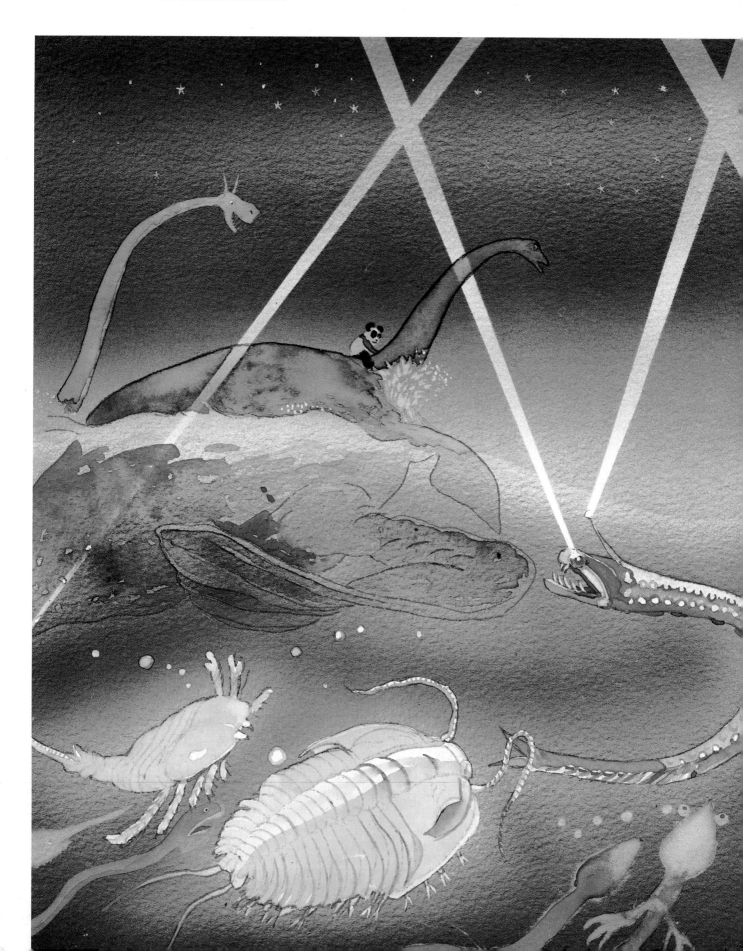

They sported and gossiped for six days and nights. They told tales of the old times when they all lived together in the ancient ocean that once covered the red land.

At dawn on the seventh day, the Bunyips said their goodbyes and swam slowly back up the rivers to their homes in the creeks and billabongs. All the sea creatures began the long journeys to their deep, secret places around the world.

"When we get home," said Lion,
"my brothers will never believe what we've seen."
"I'm not sure that *I* do," said Panda.